To my husband and best friend, Joe;
and to the fabulous four: Jeremy, Parisha, Rachel, and Ixis
—B.H.

To Cynthia Nguyen
—V.N.

The author would like to thank the Society of Children's Book Writers and Illustrators
for the Barbara Karlin Grant, which helped to complete this work.

Text copyright © 2012 by Brenda Huante
Pictures copyright © 2012 by Vincent Nguyen
All rights reserved
Distributed in Canada by D&M Publishers, Inc.
Color separations by Embassy Graphics
Printed in China by South China Printing Co. Ltd.,
Dongguan City, Guangdong Province
First edition, 2012
1   3   5   7   9   10   8   6   4   2

mackids.com

Library of Congress Cataloging-in-Publication Data
Huante, Brenda.
  Creature count : a prehistoric rhyme / Brenda Huante ; pictures by Vincent Nguyen. — 1st ed.
      p.   cm.
  Summary: Rhyming text in the pattern of "Over in the meadow" introduces dinosaurs and other
prehistoric creatures and their mothers, from one trumpeting woolly mammoth to ten hatching
maiasaurs. Includes a timeline and facts about the animals in the rhyme.
  ISBN: 978-0-374-33605-9
  [1. Stories in rhyme.   2. Dinosaurs—Fiction.   3. Prehistoric animals—Fiction.
4. Counting.]   I. Nguyen, Vincent, ill.   II. Title.

PZ8.3.H85664In 2012
[E]—dc23
                                                                        2011018835

Creature Count
A Prehistoric Rhyme

Brenda Huante

Pictures *by* Vincent Nguyen

FARRAR STRAUS GIROUX
New York

In a prehistoric meadow in the early morning sun
Lived a mother woolly mammoth and her little woolly one.
"Trumpet!" said the mother. "I trumpet!" said the one.
So they trumpeted and played in the early morning sun.

On a prehistoric mountain where the sky was so blue
Lived a mom pteranodon and her flying reptiles two.
"Soar!" said the mother. "We soar!" said the two.
So they soared through the air where the sky was so blue.

Near a prehistoric beach by the foamy green sea
Lived a mother saber-tooth and her toothy kittens three.
"Snarl!" said the mother. "We snarl!" said the three.
So they snarled and they hissed by the foamy green sea.

By a prehistoric lake on a pebble-covered shore
Lived a mom velociraptor and her little raptors four.
"Hunt!" said the mother. "We hunt!" said the four.
So they hunted in a pack on the pebble-covered shore.

In a prehistoric forest where the ferns and bushes thrived
Lived a mother stegosaur and her little armored five.
"Shake!" said the mother. "We shake!" said the five.
So they shook their bony tails where the ferns and bushes thrived.

In a prehistoric valley by the rocks and the sticks
Lived a mother T. rex and her terrible rexes six.
"Boom!" said the mother. "We boom!" said the six.
So they boomed and they thundered by the rocks and the sticks.

In a prehistoric wood where the trees reached to heaven
Lived a mom apatosaur and her little long-necks seven.
"Stretch!" said the mother. "We stretch!" said the seven.
So they stretched as they nibbled on the trees that reached to heaven.

In a prehistoric jungle where the plants grew so straight
Lived a mother hadrosaur and her crested little eight.
"Hoot!" said the mother. "We hoot!" said the eight.
So they hooted and they honked where the plants grew so straight.

Near a prehistoric swamp by a long, curling vine
Lived a mom triceratops and her frilly little nine.
"Munch!" said the mother. "We munch!" said the nine.
So they munched and they crunched the long, curling vine.

In a prehistoric nursery in her nest in a glen
Lived a mother maiasaur and her little hatchlings ten.
"Hatch!" said the mother. "We hatch!" said the ten.
So they hatched and they cuddled in their nest in a glen.

In a prehistoric meadow on a quiet, balmy night
Lived the mothers and their babies under stars that twinkled bright.
"Good night!" said the mothers. The babies said, "Sleep tight!"
And they snuggled in the moonlight of a prehistoric night.

Although the prehistoric creatures in this story are pictured together, they didn't all live at the same time. Dinosaurs and flying reptiles lived during the Mesozoic Era, 248–65 million years ago. Large early mammals—including the saber-toothed cat and the woolly mammoth—lived much later, during the Pleistocene Epoch, which was 1.8 million to 10,000 years ago.

Saber-Toothed Cat
1.8 million to 10,000 years ago

A saber-toothed cat was a meat eater that was about as large as a tiger is today. Its long canine teeth made it look very ferocious.

Woolly Mammoth
250,000–4,000 years ago

Woolly mammoths were plant eaters that probably used their long tusks to dig for plants under the snow. Their long, thick hair kept them warm and toasty in the freezing far north.

Velociraptor
84–80 million years ago

Even though these meat eaters were only as tall as your mom or dad, velociraptors hunted dinosaurs that may have been longer than your bedroom. They hunted in packs and could jump like kangaroos.

Pteranodon
86–73 million years ago

A pteranodon was not a dinosaur; it was a flying reptile. It swooped down into the water to catch fish with its long, sharp, toothless beak.

Stegosaur
155–144 million years ago

This plant eater had two rows of bony plates along its back. A stegosaur could defend itself by swinging its spiky tail.

Hadrosaur
78–74 million years ago

This plant eater was also known as a duckbill. The crested hadrosaurs had tubes in their crests that let them make loud hoots and honks.

Tyrannosaurus Rex
67–65 million years ago

Also known as T. rex, this meat eater was feared by other dinosaurs. With a head nearly as big as a refrigerator and teeth as long as bananas, it's no wonder it looked so scary!

Triceratops
67–65 million years ago

A triceratops defended itself against hungry T. rexes with its three long horns and its sharp beak. The huge frill around this plant eater's neck was made of bone.

Apatosaur
154–145 million years ago

An apatosaur was a gentle plant eater that was nearly as long as two school buses! Its long neck let it reach high into the trees for fresh leaves.

Maiasaur
80–75 million years ago

Maiasaur means "good mother lizard." This plant eater defended its eggs and hatchlings from hungry meat eaters.